Amy Ignat

The Popularity Papers 3

Words of (Questionable) Wisdom from

Lydia
Goldblatt
&
Julie
Graham-Chang

Amulet Books
New York

Weird Things That My Mom Says

Now we can cross "Living Abroad" off our Bucket List!

Apparently packing up and unpacking all of our belongings twice in less than a year is also on Mom's Bucket List.

What's a Bucket List?

It's a list of all the things that you want to do before you die.

Why is it called a Bucket List?

It's kept in a bucket?

THINGS THAT ARE HANDY ABOUT
SPRING BREAK
I can use the time to get over my jet lag now that I'm back from London.
Having a sleepover on your first night back was not a good idea.
Are you awake? Are you hungry?
Do you think Papa Dad will start making waffles soon?

We have a week off from school so Lydia can relearn how to talk American.

I am right chuffed to be home!

I genuinely can't understand most of what you just said.

That also means that we have a week to plan. And to eat burritos.

Plan?

PLAN for the REST of 6th GRADE

① Reconnect with old friends.

Even Jane. Even though Jane is dating Chuck?

Why would I care about that?

No reason. Go on.

② Not care that Jane is dating Chuck.

Not caring about something is part of your plan?

Yes, and I'm already accomplishing it.

③ Spend Spring Break studying everything that happened while I was gone so that when I get back it will be like I never left.

④ Spend Spring Break teaching Lydia how to be an American again.

If you don't start looking to the left before you cross the street, one of these days I'm going to have to scrape you off it.

While I was away, Julie made the Shih Tzus kind of mad at her, and the Bichons REALLY mad at her.

PEOPLE LYDIA SHOULD AVOID IN JUNIOR HIGH

The Bichons
(ESPECIALLY Della Dawn)

The Shih-Tzus

Chuck & Jane

The weird girl who always wears the same thing.

★ Be careful

☆ Ignore

★ Avoid

★ AVOID AT ALL COSTS !!!

THINGS I WOULD HAVE DONE DIFFERENTLY

(If Julie had left to live in London for six months) (instead of me)

① I would have stayed friends with the Shih Tzus.

Lisa   Gretchen   Jane

② I would have never let the Bichons boss me around.

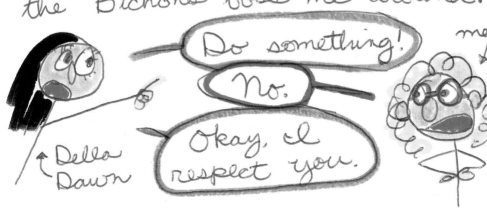

Do something!

No.

Okay, I respect you.

← Della Dawn

me ↓

③. I would have bridged the gap between the Shih Tzus and the Bichons.

And how would you have done that?

Through the calm peacemaking skills that I learned in my martial arts classes.

I thought you learned how to fight people with sticks.

That was part of it, too.

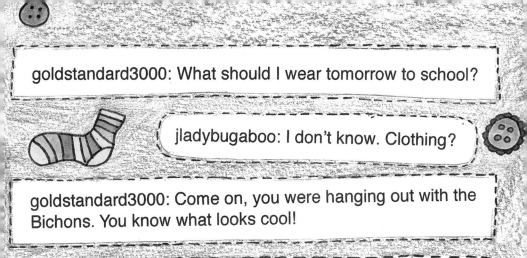

goldstandard3000: What should I wear tomorrow to school?

jladybugaboo: I don't know. Clothing?

goldstandard3000: Come on, you were hanging out with the Bichons. You know what looks cool!

jladybugaboo: The Bichons shoplifted their outfits! I don't think we want to become criminals to be fashionable like them.

goldstandard3000: I've been wearing a school uniform for the past six months!!! HELP ME!

jladybugaboo: Okay, fine, don't wear overalls. Apparently they're not cool.

goldstandard3000: I don't even own any overalls, that's your thing.

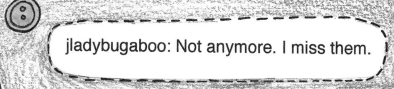

jladybugaboo: Not anymore. I miss them.

LYDIA's 1st DAY BACK!

Was shouting normal in London?

I'm going to assume that means something unpleasant.

Guess who I saw in the hallway?

Was it Roland? He's been looking for you and wants to say "Hei."

No, not Roland. I saw the Bichons.

Oh no. Did you talk to them?

No, I was in a hurry to get to class, but I totally will the next time I see them.

I really, really, really, really, really, really urge you not to.

Don't worry! It will be fine.

The Bichons are MEAN.

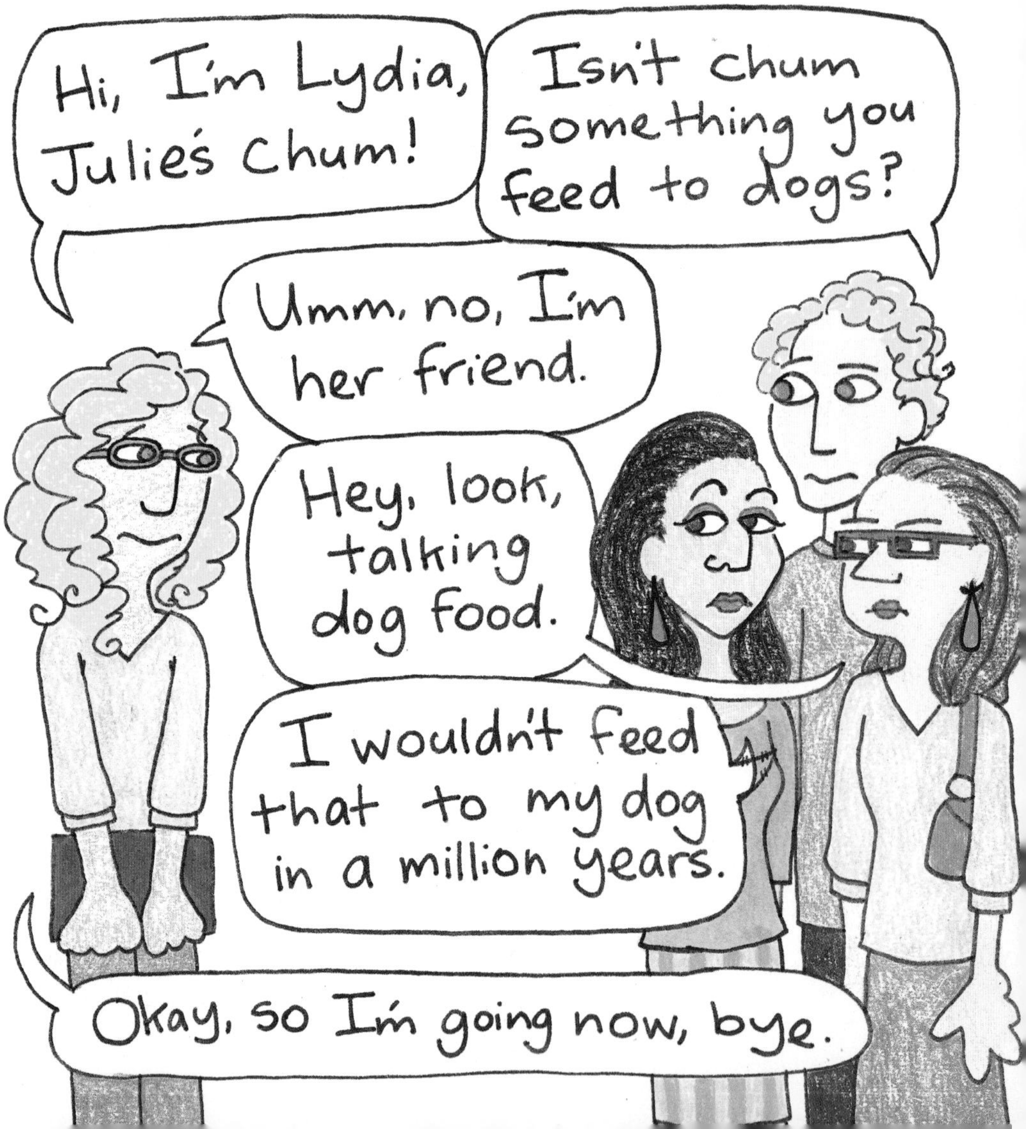

Things are much worse than I expected.

I told you, but you didn't listen.

I just assumed you were being overdramatic. We need a New Plan.

THINGS THAT WORKED in LONDON According to Lydia

① Make friends with people who might not have too many other friends.

Kids who get picked on by the Bichons

They're mean.

Kids who are embarrassed by their stutters

Kids who are maybe a little too enthusiastic about science fiction

K'plaa!

2. Form a crew and call it

OUTCASTS WEST

3. Never get picked on again! Strength in numbers!

goldstandard3000: I think that you should make friends with the arty kids.

jladybugaboo: Okay. Why?

goldstandard3000: Because we should try to make friends with lots of different people, and you're good at art, so you know their language.

jladybugaboo: I speak Art?

goldstandard3000: Sure you do. And I speak Showtunes so I can make friends with the theater people.

jladybugaboo: And I speak a little bit of Norwegian so I can make friends with the Norwegian people.

goldstandard3000: We're already friends with the Norwegian people.

jladybugaboo: Just Roland and his family. There might be more around, you never know.

Look at this page! You totally speak Art.

OPERATION SOCIAL OUTCAST

Day 1

Today is the day that Julie is going to befriend the arty kids

The art kids aren't social outcasts.

Have you seen the way they're dressed

You may have a point.

How did it go with the
arty kids?

I never got to talk to them.

Maybe you can talk to
them after school?

No, after school we're going
home. I have to tell you
something really bad that
Lisa Kovac just told me.

What?

Later.

I've never been to a
Funeral before.

I went to my great-grandmother's
funeral when I was little.
It was sad.

Do we have to go?

I think we
should. For Dukie.

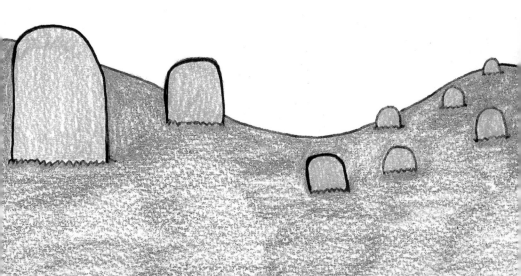

Lisa's mom is driving Lisa, Gretchen, and us to the funeral. Jane's mom isn't letting her go. We're going to drive up to New York *Not New York City, a place in New York called "Long Island"* and stay with Lisa's family there overnight, and go to the funeral in the morning.

THINGS TO PACK FOR A FUNERAL

1. Pajamas
2. Sleeping bags
3. Black clothing
4. Tissues, in case someone needs to cry, because funerals are sad
5. Black purses to put tissues in
6. Clothing to wear on the trip home
7. A tooth brush

Mom lent us black purses to put our tissues in and didn't even give us the usual lecture she gives when she lends me and Melody something.

jladybugaboo: Daddy lent me some real cloth hankies to use.

goldstandard3000: What if we have to blow our noses and get boogers all over the hankies?

jladybugaboo: Ewww. I don't know. I'll ask Papa Dad.

How big are the boogers? And what color are the boogers? Are the boogers wet or kind of crusty? This is a tough one.

jladybugaboo: Okay, Papa Dad was less than helpful. I think we should use the real tissues for the boogers and the hankies for the tears.

goldstandard3000: That makes sense.

Does anyone need a pee break?

I thought we'd all be squished in the car together, but Lisa's mom's car is enormous.

Do you remember when Daddy rented that cabin in the woods because he felt like "getting back to nature"? I think it was smaller than Lisa's mom's car. If that car had a bathroom, we could live in it.

That would be great. Mrs. Kovac can't drive for half an hour without stopping to go to the bathroom.

25

We're at Lisa's cousin's house and we're all sleeping on the floor of their teevee room. I can't sleep. I keep thinking about what Daddy said before we left—

If it's an open casket, you don't have to look if you don't want to. If you get scared, you can always politely excuse yourself and go to the bathroom and call us.

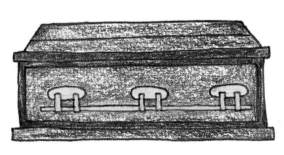

I've never even seen a closed casket.

I don't remember ever seeing Sukie's mom when she was alive, so it seems kind of weird that the one and only time I might see her is when she's dead. And what is she going to look like? I can't believe that Lydia is able to sleep. I keep hoping that she'll wake up and keep me company.

The casket was closed.

After the funeral we all went to Sukie's aunt's house. There was food on platters and flowers everywhere It was kind of like a party, only one where someone bursts into tears every once in a while. Sukie seemed happy to see us and didn't want to talk about her mom.
So how was London?
I'm right chuffed to be home.
That means Lydia's happy to be back. She's still adjusting.

It felt good to be there for Sukie, but I was nervous about what to say. Me, too.

In London the trunk of a car is called "the boot."

I drew a picture of Lydia looking like a ninja.

I just couldn't stop thinking about what if something happens to one of my dads.

Me, too, except I was thinking about my mom and Melody.

We got home from Long Island pretty late, but Daddy and Papa Dad were both waiting up for me. I was so happy to see them.

Promise to never, ever die.

We can't make that promise, Sweetie.

But we promise that we'll always be with you, no matter what.

We plan to turn into ghosts and spy on you, so you'll pretty much have to be good all the time.

PAPA DAD!!

I gnore your father.

From: sukiejaithoms100
To: jladybugaboo, goldstandard3000

Hi guys,

The card you guys made me was so nice! I'm going to guess that Julie drew it (no offense, Lydia, but I've seen your drawings...). I just wanted to say Hi and Thanks because it really did make me feel better.

Love,
Sukie

From: jladybugaboo
To: sukiejaithoms100, goldstandard3000

We just wanted to make sure that you know you'll always have friends here and that we're thinking about you.

From: goldstandard3000
To: sukiejaithoms100, jladybugaboo

Wait, are you saying that my art isn't the bestest thing you've ever seen in your life? I am deeply offended!

From: jladybugaboo
To: sukiejaithoms100, goldstandard3000

Ignore her.

From: sukiejaithoms100
To: jladybugaboo, goldstandard3000

Okay!

From: goldstandard3000
To: sukiejaithoms100, jladybugaboo

Harrumph!!!!!!!

goldstandard3000: I'm so freaked out that something is going to happen to Mom and I don't want to be away from her.

jladybugaboo: I'm the same way about my dads!

goldstandard3000: I don't even like having Melody away from me for too long.

jladybugaboo: I caught Papa Dad putting extra salt on his dinner and I actually slapped his hand.

I think we're going to go crazy if we keep worrying all the time.

I don't know what else to do.

We <u>have</u> to focus on something else.

I've been thinking some more.

Uh-oh.

I think we've been too worried about what other people think about us.

We?

Okay, **ME**. But I think I'm tired of worrying about what other people think about us, and after what happened to Sukie's mom, I think that there are more important things to care about.

MORE IMPORTANT THINGS TO CARE ABOUT
1. OUR FAMILIES
But if we spend too much time thinking about all of the bad things that could happen to them, we're going to go crazy.
How are those sharks able to swim in lava?
This seems both highly unlikely and very unpleasant!

2. OUR FRIENDS

We still have friends and we haven't spent enough time with them.

3. OUR FUTURE

Think about it — we'll be turning thirteen over the summer. We'll be teenagers, which is practically like being an adult.

An adult that can't legally drive or vote.

But we can make our own decisions about our own lives. We've spent too much time worrying about what people will think about us. It's time to just do what we want to do.

What exactly do we want to do?

Possible future alien invasion

Take this seriously!!

THE TRUNK LIST

1. Star in the school musical. *Me.* Definitely not me.

2. Stay up all night.

3. Show Ms. Harrington something so impressive that she'll be forced to say, "What you have done is unquestionably great, Julie!"

4. Be friends with Chuck again without it being all weird.

5. Go skydiving.

Why is skydiving on our list?
It was on my mom's Bucket List and I thought it looked cool.

I'm crossing it off our list. I'm also finding your mom's list and crossing it off that, too.

I just emailed our Trunk List to Sukie, and she wrote back pretty fast.

From: sukiejaithoms100
To: jladybugaboo

Sounds like an interesting list, but don't get disappointed if you can't do everything on it, because kids don't have a whole lot of control over what they can and can't do.

At first, when we started talking about the Trunk List, I thought that Lydia was just trying to distract us from worrying all the time, but now I want to prove to Sukie that we can achieve our goals, and she can achieve hers, too, as long as her goals aren't totally crazy. You already crossed skydiving off the list. Let it go.

STAR in SCHOOL MUSICAL

In order to get a starring role in the musical, I have to audition.

(PROBLEM) You missed the audition for the musical when you were living in London.

SOLUTION: Audition anyway!

How? Are you going to just march into the director's office and sing?

I demand an audience with you!

And... you are...?

TRA LA LA LA!!!

Guess what I just did!

You marched into the director's office and started singing?

Exactly!

Wait, what? I was joking. Joking with the jokes. Ha ha, joking.

But I did it, and he's going to give me a part in the musical!

Oh my gosh, Congratulations!!!

THE MUSIC MAN starring LYDIA!

1ST ITEM ON OUR TRUNK LIST
ACCOMPLISHED!

Okay, so it's not the lead, but I get to sing the line "In March I got a gray mackinaw" all by myself!

What's a mackinaw?

I think it's a kind of bird.

My first rehearsal is after school today.

Wish me luck!

From: jladybugaboo
To: sukiejaithoms100

Lydia got a part in <u>The Music Man</u> just like she wanted!
She just walked right up to the director and said, "I want to
audition for the musical," and then she just started to sing,
and now she has a solo about wanting a mackinaw, which
she thinks is a kind of bird. Isn't that great?

Papa Dad and Daddy wanted me to tell you that if you ever
want to come for a visit, you can stay with us.

From: sukiejaithoms100
To: jladybugaboo

Wow, tell her congratulations for me. Also, my aunt thinks
that a mackinaw is a kind of a coat.

I can't come to stay anytime soon because I don't want to
leave my aunt right now. She's really sad and she needs me.
But maybe sometime over the summer?

jladybugaboo: How did rehearsal go?
goldstandard3000: Good, I guess.
jladybugaboo: Did you get to sing your line?
goldstandard3000: Yeah, but no one welcomed me to the cast or congratulated me on my moxie. Maybe they're just intimidated by talent.
jladybugaboo: Maybe they were intimidated by something else. Did you threaten to stick-fight with anyone?
goldstandard3000: Of course not! Do you think I've developed an intimidating warrior stance without realizing it?
jladybugaboo: No, I was just making fun of you.

During rehearsal today one of the other cast members, Emily, stepped on my foot. She said it was an accident, but I was pretty sure that she did it on purpose because it felt like she put a lot of force into it. I was about to confront her about it when this guy, Jake, told me why she didn't like me.

If it weren't for **you**, Emily would be singing the line about the mackinaw. I wouldn't try to be friends with her if I were you. Or anyone else here.

goldstandard3000: How am I supposed to get stuff on the Trunk List done if I have to be worried about Emily's feelings? Besides, she has another line about getting raisins from Fresno, so it's not like I'm destroying her theater career. I wish all the other cast members could see that.

jladybugaboo: It's okay, because we still have friends, remember? Want to go to the skate park to meet up with Roland?

Want to stand up?

Nope!

While Roland helped Lydia learn how to skateboard, Jon told me about how if you take Advanced Art in 8th grade, you get to do an independent study project.

I'm going to draw a comic book and my dad is going to photocopy it at his office so that I can give it away on Free Comic Book Day.

And then he asked me if I want to help him!

Ms. Harrington's 8th Grade Art
Independent Study Project Guidelines

1. The Independent Study Project will count for 50% of the Artist's spring semester final grade.

2. The ISP (Independent Study Project) idea will be discussed with Ms. Harrington in advance of beginning the project.

3. The Artist must submit a typed, double-spaced plan to Ms. Harrington for approval before embarking on his/her ISP.

4. The Artist may receive assistance on his/her ISP as long as:
   a. the person assisting receives proper credit;
   b. the work of the person assisting does not exceed the work of the Artist;
   c. all major ideas are originated by the Artist.

5. The Artist must hand in a completed project no later than two weeks before the end of the scholastic year.

That's me!!!

When Ms. Harrington sees me doing work on an 8th grade level, she'll definitely be forced to say,

Or something like that. Something else for the Trunk! We're ripping through these. We should come up with some more things we want to do.

COMIC BOOK RESEARCH

Today after school Jonathan took me to a comic book store to show me how he wants his comic book to look.

goldstandard3000: How's the research going?

jladybugaboo: Okay, I guess.

goldstandard3000: I'm sure that Della Dawn is really jealous that you get to work with Jonathan on his project.

jladybugaboo: She shouldn't be. He's not the easiest person to work with.

goldstandard3000: Is he being mean?

jladybugaboo: No, I just don't really understand what he wants.

What about a vampire getting smashed in the head with a skateboard and one of the splinters

From the board hits him in the EYE, but he's still alive, but in a kind of a dead way, 'cause he's a vampire. You can draw that, right?

Bonk!

Lisa just saw my drawing and asked why the skateboarder was attacking the guy with weird teeth. This is hard.

BREAKDOWN of CARTOONING DUTIES

What Jon does:
1. Practices skateboarding
2. Draws skateboarding vampires
3. Comes up with new ways to kill vampires
4. Gives Constructive Criticism

What Julie does:
1. Comes up with storylines
2. Draws the Comic book
3. Redraws the Comic book when Jon has a new idea
4. Gets Snacks

We've been working really hard. Time for a snack break?

I was talking to Roland
in the hall and he wants us
to come with him to the movies
on Saturday. His brother Anders
is going, and so is Melody.

I have no time! The comic book
has to be finished by Sunday
night. I could go, if Jon did any
work. WHICH HE DOES NOT.

Maybe Roland and I could help?
Sure, if you come up with a totally
new story and help me to draw it.

I have some ideas....

Lydia's
thinking face

New Story Ideas

LYDIA'S IDEAS

You need action in your comic book, so I suggest having lots of ninjas in it. You're always drawing me fighting like a ninja, so I know you can do it (even though I would only ever use my martial arts skills for defense, thank you very much).

ROLAND'S IDEAS

Roland keeps making troll suggestions. He knows tons of Norwegian folktales and most of them involve a bunch of trolls.

The meaner and stronger a troll is, the more heads he has.

So a super mean troll would have...

Nine heads.

That is super goofy.

I think you mean "extra scary."

According to Roland, most Norwegian stories are about a boy named "Ash Lad" who saves three princesses from three different trolls after two of his brothers have failed to do the same thing.

But why does everything have to happen three times?

Because that is how it is!

It seems a little bit repetitive.

Troll skal atter herske.

I like drawing aliens so we should definitely throw some of them into the story, too. Definitely.

Guru Sukie vs. Halvor

An Ash Lady Adventure

Once upon a time there were a group of girl ninjas called the Ash Ladies. They all lived and trained together under the guidance of their leader, Guru Sukie. One day their island fortress was attacked by a three-headed troll named Halvor, and Guru Sukie was kidnapped. Halvor took Guru Sukie back to his castle and made plans to eat her because he thought that would help him to gain her guru powers, which included superwisdom and also the ability to turn into any kind of animal for five minutes whenever she ate cheese. Unfortunately, Halvor was lactose intolerant so there was no cheese in his castle. But because she was super wise, Guru Sukie knew that her Ash Ladies were going to save her.

The Ash Ladies loaded up their hovercraft to get to Halvor's castle, but were stopped by an alien spaceship. After a mighty battle, the Ash Ladies overtook the spaceship just to find out that it was run by very friendly aliens who were only shooting tickle rays at them because they wanted to be friends.

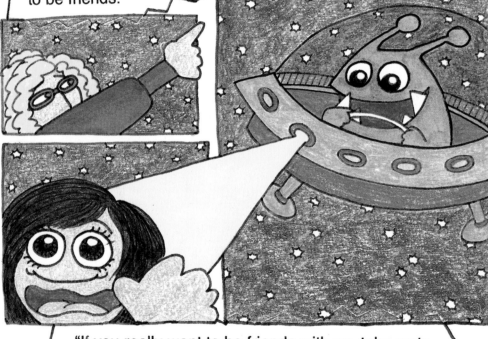

"If you really want to be friends with us, take us to Halvor's castle!" said the Ash Ladies, and after the friendly aliens had loaded the address into their GPS system, they all flew there.

To the Ash Ladies' surprise, the castle was guarded by skateboarding vampires, but the Ash Ladies kicked them and then they died. Then there was a huge battle between Halvor and the Ash Ladies, which they won by throwing cheese at him. He had an allergic reaction, and then Guru Sukie ate some cheese, became a bee, and stung Halvor, who had another allergic reaction and died. And then Guru Sukie and the Ash Ladies went to live on the alien planet as part of a cultural-exchange program.

And now we have a story!
Roland is a little disappointed that I gave Halvor only three heads, but there's no way I'm drawing nine heads every time he has a scene.

Daddy promised to get pizza for us tomorrow, and Papa Dad promised to bug us only a little bit.

Is Roland still coming?

Yes, but his mom is picking him up at 10. He might come over again on Sunday to help if we're not finished.

What about Jon?

He said he's really busy but he'll try to make some time.

We're totally going to get this comic book done in time. Don't even worry. I've got a secret weapon.

Should I be worried?

Of course not!

Maybe.

A little.

3 A.M.!!!!

THIS STAYING UP ALL NIGHT TO GET WORK DONE WAS A GREAT IDEA!!!

I never knew what three o'clock in the morning looked like before!

WE ARE GETTING SO MUCH WORK DONE!!!!

We should do this all the time!

YOU SHOULD USE MORE EXCLAMATION POINTS!!!

I can't believe we slept until two in the afternoon.

We missed waffles? Why didn't you wake us up?

But it was worth it! We finished the comic book! Except for the cover, but Jon is going to do that before his dad photocopies it. Jon said that they're going to bring a big stack to the school so everyone can see what we did. So excited.

The Ash Lady Adventures

By Jonathan Cravens

With Julie Gramchan

I'm not super happy with the cover, but I guess it's Jon's comic book so he can do what he wants.

Has Ms. Harrington seen it yet?

I don't know. I'm kind of nervous that she won't like it.

Why? It looks great! Except for maybe the cover, which fails to acknowledge my valuable contributions.

Ninjas and coffee?

Exactly.

I acknowledge you!

Certificate
of
Awesomeness
for
NINJAS
and
COFFEE

That's bette

Roland is kind of upset about the comic book.

Why is a vampire eating a ninja? There's no part in the book where that happens. It makes no sense. And my name isn't in the book, and neither is Lydia's, and who is Julie Gramchan?

I wish his name was on the book, but Jon and his dad already brought them to the store and the school. I even sent one to Jukie. Am I supposed to find every copy and add Roland's name with a marker?

Everyone is talking about the comic! I heard Gretchen and Lisa talking about it, and Devon was reading it, and did I tell you that Chuck thinks it's really cool?

That's great. Did you talk to Roland?

Yes.

So what did he say?

He may need a little more time to cool off.

Are you still mad?

Luftputebåten min er full av ål!

Maybe you need more time to cool off.

THE REVIEWS ARE IN!

Everything is working out! By doing what we most wanted to do, we've become popular! We should just keep doing whatever we put in the Trunk. We are living our lives to the fullest and it is working!

TROUBLE.

Your comic book is really cute.
Thanks, Della Dawn.
I can't believe you made Jane into a troll.
What? No I didn't.
Oh, everyone knows it's Jane. It's really funny.

Do you think they look alike?

Of course not! Jane has only one he

Seriously, do you think the head c the right looks like Jane?

Jane doesn't have a beard.

But it kind of looks like her.

Okay, maybe a little, but I'm sure that Della Dawn is the only one who's noticed.

The Ash Lady Adventures is so great! I love that the guru is named Sukie and that one of the Halvor heads looks like Jane. She must think it's hysterical.

I bet you think you're soooo funny with your little comic book, but soon everyone is going to know that you're just a HUGE JERK.

And You are an even BIGGER JERK.

I'm pretty sure Jane doesn't think it's hysterical.

jladybugaboo: What are we going to do?

goldstandard3000: I think that the comic book speaks for itself, and if anyone wants to interpret it in a stupid way, that's their problem.

We have a problem.

The cast of The Music Man thinks the comic book is about them. How was I supposed to know that three of them are lactose intolerant?

New Problem

Ms. Harrington wants a meeting with Jon and me. At first I was kind of excited because I thought she'd be congratulating us on a job well done, but Jon was worried.

If Ms. Harrington asks you if I worked on the comic book, you have to tell her the truth.

Which is...

Of course I did! The whole thing was my idea!

Oh, okay.

How did it go with Ms. Harrington?

Okay, I guess. She asked a bunch of questions and Jon did most of the talking.

What did he say?

Mostly stuff about how he came up with the story and helped me to design the look of everything and how he's always been a fan of traditional Norwegian folklore.

So... he lied.

Pretty much. He thanked me afterward for keeping quiet.

What a prince.

Tonight is the opening night of The Music Man, and the rest of the cast is still less than friendly to Lydia.

I am going to be so glad when this is over. Everyone keeps calling me "Solo Thief".

WHO NEEDS A STUPID CAST PARTY ANYWAY?

It seems like the other cast members forgot to tell Lydia that there was going to be a cast party after the show at Emily's house, but it doesn't matter because we're going to hang out all night and watch movies and try to say stuff we've found in our Norwegian phrase book. Who needs to go to a stupid party when we have hours of Norwegian fun ahead of us?

Jeg må øve pa norsken min.

A Brand-New Morning!

We've decided we're not going to care about mean actors or people who misinterpret innocent comic books. They're jerks and life is too short for jerks! Plus the musical is over, and most of the cast were 8th graders so I won't have to deal with them next year anyway.

The school year is over in just two months, so all we have to do is lie low and we'll be fine. Better than fine, because we've still achieved awesome stuff on our

TRUNK LIST.

Have you seen it yet?

I don't know what you're talking about, but guess what? Chuck just saw me in the hallway and asked if I was going to martial arts camp. It's two weeks in the summer of intense martial arts training. Isn't that cool?

Have you been to the bathroom?

That seems like sort of a personal question, but no, I haven't. Do you think my mom would let me go to martial arts camp?

I saw something not good in the bathroom.

What was it? Is it smelly? Do I want to know?

Probably not, but we should go look at it after class anyway.

What the wall
of the Girls'
Bathroom is
supposed to
look like

What it looks
like right now

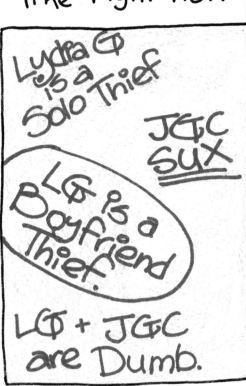

Lydia G.
is a
Solo Thief

JGC
SUX

LG is a
Boyfriend
Thief.

LG + JGC
are Dumb.

What boyfriend did I steal?
Why would they say we're dumb?
How can I be dumb and a
boyfriend thief and a solo thief?
This is some confusing graffiti.
What are we going to do?

The other janitors are never going to believe this.
LG is a Boyfriend Thief.
JGC sux!
LG + JGC are Dumb
Can I take a photo with my cell phone to show them?
NO!

After the Janitor was done making fun of us, she told us tha it's impossible to wash permanent ink off, and we'd just have to live with the graffiti until the bathrooms are repainted over th summer.

I hate it. I hate it SO MUCE

I wonder if anything is written in the Boys' Bathroom.

What if there is? What would say? If Roland still talked to he'd tell us. Can you ask Chuck? How would I even begin to bring up that conversation?

So, this martial arts camp sounds great! Speaking of martial arts, is there anything weird written about Julie or me in the Boys' Bathroom?

I found out that there isn't anything written about us on the Boys' Bathroom walls.

Did you talk to Chuck?

No, I asked Jamie Burke to take a look for me. He said that there wasn't anything, but then he offered to write something. I had to wrestle the marker away from him.

GOLDBLATT AND GRAHAM-CHANG

PRIVATE EYES

We spent all last year observing and figuring out the Shih-Tzus. We're practically already detectives. We should be able to figure out who is writing mean stuff about us on the Girls' Bathroom walls.

LIST OF POSSIBLE SUSPECTS

1. Emily, because she's mad at Lydia for stealing her solo. I didn't.

2. Jane, because she thinks we made her into a troll

3. Anyone who is really sensitive about being lactose intolerant

MORE SUSPECTS

4. Roland, because he's mad at me for stealing his ideas, even though I didn't mean to (but he's an unlikely suspect because he probably doesn't spend a whole lot of time in the Girls' Bathroom)

5. Della Dawn, because she doesn't like either of us. *And she thinks you stole Jonathan from her.* She can have him!

6. MYSTERY PERSON, because we accidentally stepped on her/his foot one time or something like that

I don't like you.

I didn't realize we had so many enemies. *Me, neither.*

A CLOSER OBSERVATION OF WHAT WAS WRITTEN

> ## Lydia G. is a Solo Thief.

I'm so tired of people saying that. It was ONE LINE and I didn't STEAL IT, it was given to me by the director, so whoever wrote that has to be in the musical.

> ## JGC Sux.

I think whoever wrote that was trying to say that I "suck" but they don't know how to spell. I think they spelled it "sux" on purpose, to save time.

Well, that's just lazy. Whoever wrote that is lazy.

LG is a BOYFRIEND THIEF

How can I be a boyfriend thief if I don't have a boyfriend? And whose boyfriend did I steal? What's more, how can you steal a human being?

I guess you could ambush them and then keep them in a locked cage.

1. That's not stealing, that's kidnapping.

B. That's kind of creepy.

I was just trying to answer your question.

Even if I was a big crazy kidnapper, that's not the same thing as being a boyfriend thief.

Quit squirming!

Why did you draw Chuck? No reason.

LG AND JCG ARE Dumb

If they're trying to insult u this is really weak.
I'm pretty unimpressed.
I mean, if you're going to be a big bad vandal, at least don't be boring about it.
We could do so much better.

So we have a suspect who is lazy, boring, and in the musical.

Maybe we should just ignore the graffiti. Even if we found out who wrote it, what would we do? Be really, really mad at them?

So you don't think there's anything that we can do.

I don't think that a person who would write such stupid stuff about anyone is worth it.

Dear Lydia,

Greetings from sunny London! Ha Ha, you know it's not sunny here! How are you? Everything is good here. Becca went to Scotland on holiday and bought you a load of yarn. I couldn't decide what colour you'd like so I bought a heap. So we thought we'd send it to you along with some goodies. Write to us, we miss you!

Love,

Delilah, Becca, Henry, + Nabil

P.s. Victoria has been telling everyone that she's going to stay with you in your mansion in the States. She's _barking_ _mad_!

goldstandard3000: I just got a package from London!

jladybugaboo: From the Outcasts?

goldstandard3000: Yes! They sent me all sorts of goodies and Becca got me yarn from her vacation in Scotland. It's all soft and fluffy. And they sent you some of the chocolate eggs with surprise toys in them.

jladybugaboo: I love those!!!

goldstandard3000: The Outcasts are the best.

jladybugaboo: Do you miss them?

goldstandard3000: More than I thought I would. I had so many friends there. What are we doing wrong here?

Trunk List, PROS and CONS

PROS

We did almost everything on the list

① I was in the school musical (even though I missed the auditions

② Ms. Harrington was really impressed with my cartooning.

This is unbelievable!

③ We stayed up all night.

CONS

There were some consequences that we really didn't expect.

① Nobody else who was in the musical thought I should be there.

② Jonathan got all the credit for our work and Roland is mad at me. Also, everyone thought the comic book was about them and is super-graffiti mad at both of us.

③ We missed out on waffles when we stayed up all night.

So the only thing on our Trunk List that we didn't do is to be friends with Chuck again.
But he did think the comic book was cool.
Do you want to try to be friends with him again?
I don't know. It seems like every time we accomplish something on the Trunk List, something else happens that makes us totally unpopular.
Maybe the Trunk List is

CURSED.

Grrr!
Arrg!

May

You will not believe what I just saw in the hallway!

Was it a bear?

No. Why would I see a bear in the hallway?

I was just thinking of things you could say you saw that you totally wouldn't believe.

What Lydia Actually Saw—
YOU DON'T CARE ABOUT HOW I FEEL ABOUT ANYTHING!
Do you think they're breaking up?

Telltale Signs That a Couple is BREAKING UP

1. Arguing a lot.

Blah Blah Blah Anger!

Blah blah more anger!

2. Complaining to other people about arguing a lot.

He totally doesn't care how I feel about anything!

Blah Blah Sympathy.

3. The guy packs his stuff and leaves.

That's pretty telltale.

CONFIRMATION!

Jane told Lisa

who told Alexis

who told Ben

who told Maxine

who told us

that Jane and Chuck broke up.

goldstandard3000: Jane and Chuck didn't break up.

jladybugaboo: But Maxine told me that Ben told her that Alexis told him that Lisa told her that Jane and Chuck broke up.

goldstandard3000: Well, I saw Chuck after school and he told me that they didn't, but that she's mad at him.

jladybugaboo: Why?

goldstandard3000: Because she hates me and he's friends with me.

jladybugaboo: Oh. So if he stays friends with you, she stays mad at him?

goldstandard3000: I guess so.

So I just wanted you to know that just because I'm not going to be talking to you again doesn't mean we're not friends.
Oh. But you're talking to me right now.
Yeah, but this is the last time.
Can we communicate through a series of elaborate hand gestures?
Probably not.

So there's no way that you can be friends with Chuck again?

Not while he's dating Jane. Oh, and you can't be friends with him either, because she hates you for putting the Jane Troll into the comic book.

I figured as much. This is so lame.

I think we need a different plan.

Oh, no. No no no no no. I thought our plan was to get through the rest of the school year nicely and quietly without doing anything dramatic that could make us somehow even less popular than we already are.

We can't possibly be any less popular, so we've got nothing to lose.

You make a depressing point.

From: sukiejaithoms100
To: jladybugaboo

Jane can be unreasonable sometimes. Tell Lydia not to worry too much about it—she'll cool down eventually. Hopefully!

Tomorrow my aunt and I are going to be in a breast cancer walkathon. We've been in training for a while and she's worse than Coach Tkaczuk! I'll let you know if my feet fall off.

At least Sukie sounds like she's okay.

It's really nice that she's in the walkathon. I'd be in a walkathon.

Maybe we should train for one.

Actually, this gives me an idea.

I think that we need a

NEW TRUNK LIST.

What did all of the things on our Trunk List have in common?

They contained both words and numbers. And sometimes drawings.

They were all selfish. It was all stuff we wanted to do for ourselves.

But we wanted to live our lives to the fullest.

I think we can do that in a better way.

What way?

We can **DO GOOD.**

NEW PLAN

GOOD WORKS

We will do things to help other peop
That way not so many people will
want to write mean things about
us on the bathroom walls.
Maybe people will want to writ
nice things about us on the
bathroom walls.

We don't want that, because it's still
defacing public property!
Hey, if it's nice, I'm calling it art

Lydia is
a good
person!

Julie is
very nice!!

THE NEW AND IMROVED
TRUNK LIST

①. Feed the hungry.

②. Clothe the poor.

③. Be kind to people with no friends.

④. Make sure that Roland gets credit for his work.

If we spend our whole lives doing good things for other people, no one would hate us anymore.

You've had worse ideas.

I certainly have.

us, being ngelically good

where's my harp?

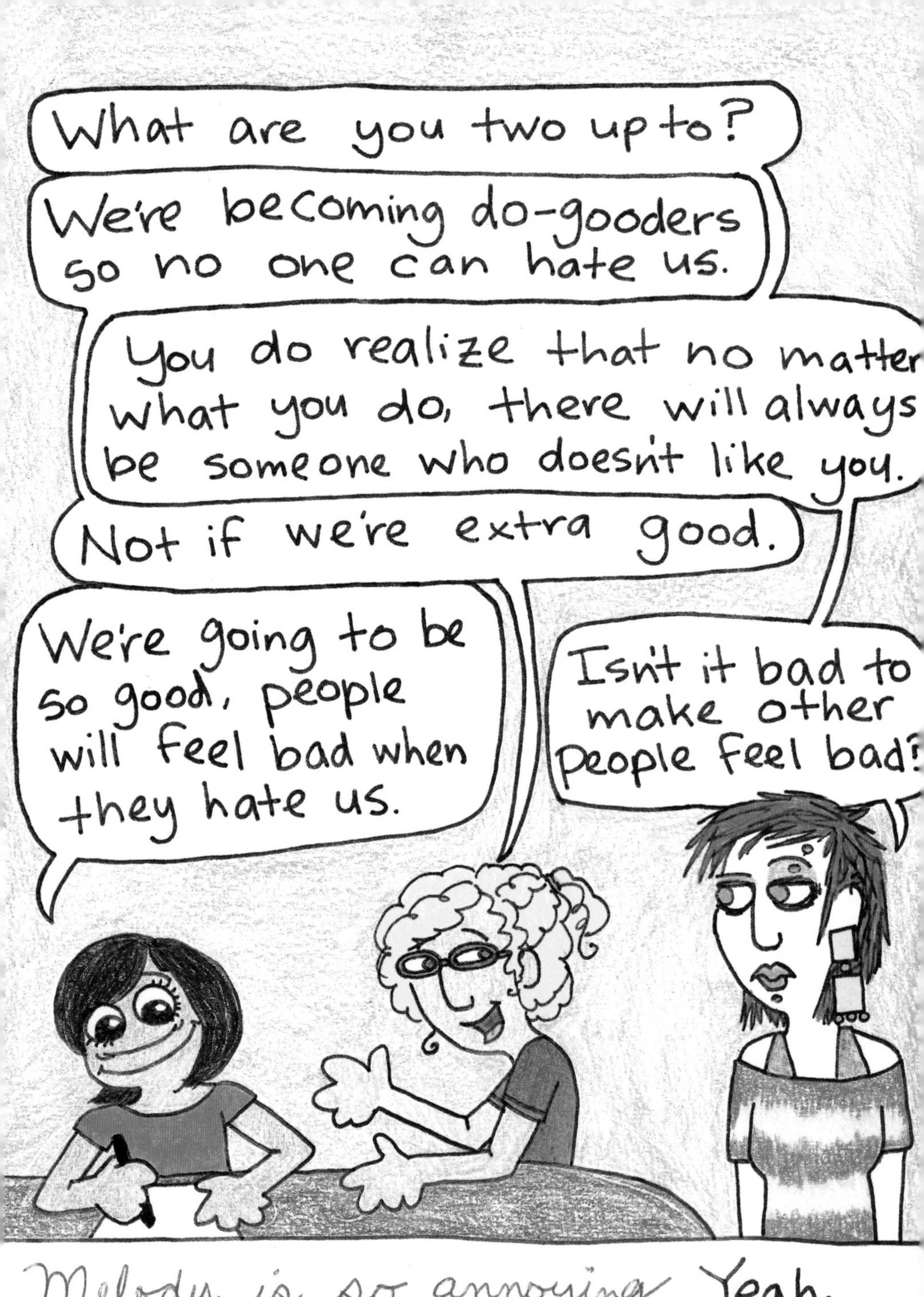

Melody is so annoying. Yeah.

MELODY'S ANNOYING SUGGESTION

If you guys want to do good things for other people, you can help me knit hats for cancer patients. Sometimes the treatment for cancer can make the patients' hair fall out, so there are organizations that give nice, soft hats to them.

Materials: 1 100 Gm. Skein of yarn, and a set of double pointed needles, size 7 (or those needed to achieve gauge)

Gauge: 5 stitches = 1 inch in stockinette stitch

Directions: Loosely cast on 100 (110) stitches. Divide them evenly between three of the needles. Begin knitting in the round, being careful not to twist the stitches. Work in stockinette stitch for 6.5" (7").

In the next round, begin decreasing as follows:

Round 1: (Knit 8, Knit 2tog) around.

Round 2 and all even rounds: Knit.

Round 3: (Knit 7, Knit 2tog) around.

Round 5: (Knit 6, Knit 2tog) around.

Round 7: (Knit 5, Knit 2tog) around.

Round 9: (Knit 4, Knit 2tog) around.

Round 11: (Knit 3, Knit 2tog) around.

Round 13: (Knit 2, Knit 2tog) around.

Round 15: (Knit 1, Knit 2tog) around.

Round 17: Knit 2tog around.

Cut the yarn, leaving a 15" tail, weave it through the stitches remaining, and fasten off.

Melody's suggestion is nice and all, but I only know how to knit scarves, and hats are totally different from scarves.

hat
↙(very different from) scarf

Do cancer patients need scarves? Maybe you can make cancer scarves? How is a scarf going to help a bald person?

What?

You're kidding, right?

We should probably stick to our original New and Improved Trunk List.

From: sukiejaithoms100
To: jladybugaboo

Hey girlie,

New York is soooooo pretty right now! You and Goldy HAVE to come and visit sometime soon. Gretchen and Lisa visited last weekend, and I know you guys aren't really hanging out anymore, but still it would great if we could all be together again. How are you doing? Is Goldy still talking British?

Sukie

From: jladybugaboo
To: sukiejaithoms100

We're okay--Lydia is mostly understandable, although she still says "crisps" when she means "potato chips."

How was the walkathon? Did you make it to the finish line? Lydia and I have decided that instead of only doing what we want to do, we're going to become philanthropists. We want to do things that make people happy, like feeding the hungry and clothing the poor and stuff.

From: sukiejaithoms100
To: jladybugaboo

That sounds neat. Maybe you guys can come to New York and do the walkathon with us next year? I think by then I might be able to feel my feet again...

How To FEED the HUNGRY

Every year at Thanksgiving the Goldblatts and Graham-Changs volunteer at a food pantry.

But that's just one day a year! We can do more!

They're all 8th graders and they're always complaining about how hungry they are. And it would benefit everyone if they shut up for a minute. This sounds like a job for...

Look, you can draw superheroes after all

We spent most of the day making cookies to bring in to school tomorrow. Daddy has a cookbook with low-calorie recipes in it, so we picked one and substituted all the low-fat ingredients with high-fat ingredients so that the Hungry Girls will finally feel full.

OUR PLAN FOR
COOKIE DISTRIBUTION

Usually when someone brings baked goods into school for a bake sale or something, suddenly they are surrounded by everyone who wants a free cookie.

Maybe we should just give them to everyone. Then people will definitely like us.

No, we're following the Trunk List! We're going to wrap them up in little paper bags and give them to the people who need them the most, in a sneaky way.

It's going to be great to not have to hear how hungry they are for one day!

So we thought we were doing great, until...

Jamie, where did you get those cookies?

From the trash. Don't worry, they were in a bag. Want one?

First of all, WHY WOULD JAMIE EAT SOMETHING OUT OF THE GARBAGE? And why were the cookies in the garbage in the first place? I don't know which is more upsetting.

I don't get it. They were so hungry. Now I'm hungry, thinking about all those poor, mostly uneaten cookies.

Does it count if we're hungry and we feed ourselves?

Probably not.

Have you been to the bathroom today?

You are entirely too occupied with the progress of my bladder.

No, doofus, there's new graffiti in the bathroom.

Oh no. What does it say now?

MYSTERY!

First someone wrote mean things about us in the bathroom.
Then ~~someone~~ covered up those mean things with flowers and stuff. I wish we had thought to do that.
It's still graffiti. But who did it? Someone arty?

But we don't know any of them. Why would they be nice to us?

We don't know who it was, but someone did something nice for us by covering up the graffiti, so now we need to do something nice for someone else.

And then, a few years later...

I don't know if things are going to work out exactly like this, but it's worth a try.

TRUNK LIST ITEM #2
CLOTHING the POOR

Since we can't afford to go out and buy new clothing, we're going to donate some of our nicer clothing to someone who really needs it.

And from what we've observed, no one needs it more than Jen Mattocks.

dark colors

ripped clothing

unmatching

kind of dirty

Also, it looks like we're the same size and it's a good way to get rid of the clothing that the Bichons stole for me.

PROBLEM: How to Get the Clothing to Jen

jladybugaboo: I think we made a mistake by just giving the cookies to the Hungry Girls. Maybe they thought that we were giving them charity and they were offended.

goldstandard3000: That's ridiculous. Cookies aren't offensive.

jladybugaboo: Still, I think we have to be careful about giving clothing to Jen. We don't want her to feel bad about being poor. We need to find a way to help her without her knowing that we're helping her.

goldstandard3000: But how will we get credit for helping Jen if no one knows that we helped her?

jladybugaboo: We might not get credit. But we'll still be helping, so that's good, right?

goldstandard3000: I guess so.

OUR PLAN (#8,347)

1.) Become friends with Jen.

Problem: Jen isn't very friendly.

We're going to find out what Jen likes so it will be easier for us to become friends with her. After we're friends, we can find a way to get the clothing to her without looking like we pity her.

Looks like we're back to observing and recording.

Observations of
JEN MATTOCKS

①. Jen is in 7th grade, but doesn't hang out with other 7th graders.

②. This is because Jen is always alone. Which is good, because she probabl wants friends and we're available.

③. Jen likes listening to music.

④. Jen likes reading books.

⑤. Other people are mean to Jen.

Hey, look, it's Jenny Mad Dogs.

Grr.

What a freak.

⑥. Jen doesn't seem to care when other people are mean to her.

We need music to listen to.
I can borrow Melody's headphones.
Great! And we have plenty of books, so all we need to do is sit near Jen while reading and listening to music.
So if we sit in silence next to her, that will make us friends?

Hello, I see you are reading and listening to music. So are we!

Hooray! Let's be friends.

You do realize that it never works out like you predict in your drawings.

So things were going as planned.

It's too bad that the high school is right next to the junior high.

I may have neglected to tell Melody that I was borrowing her headphones.

Why I Will Not Take Melody Goldblatt's Things Without Asking

by Lydia Goldblatt

Taking things from someone without asking permission is wrong, even if you're taking things from your own sister. If you take your sister's things, she might miss her bus to school because she is too busy looking for the things that you took. If that happens, she might have to take her bike to school when she is probably not wearing bicycle-appropriate clothing. So she might have to waste more time changing into bicycle-appropriate clothing, which was probably not what she wanted to wear because she's very deliberate about her fashion choices. This will probably make your sister really, really angry, especially when she's really late to school and is given a demerit for tardiness. None of this would have happened if her inconsiderate sister hadn't taken her thing without asking, so her inconsiderate sister will never, ever, ever, never do that sort of thing again, and is very, very, very grateful that Melody will not tell Mom about it.

Sorry sorry sorry sorry sorry sorry,

Lydia

Guess who I just talked to.

Roland?

No, Jen! She said

It sucks that your sister is so mean.

Then I told her about how Melody made me write an essay that she'll show to Mom if she gets mad again. Jen thought it was funny.

It is kind of funny. So are you friends now?

Yes! We're going to hang out after school at your house.

My house? Why my house?

Because the clothes are at your house. Also, the less Melody sees me, the safer I am from her wrath.

THINGS WE NOW KNOW ABOUT OUR NEW FRIEND JEN

1. Jen is a Vegan, which means that she won't eat meat or dairy or anything that comes from an animal. She won't even eat honey because it comes from bees!
2. Jen's older brother is in a band.
3. Jen's parents don't eat dinner with her! She has to find stuff in the fridge and cook for herself.

We came up with an excuse to give Jen the stolen Bichon clothing.

You know, you look like you're the same size as me.

Hey, we should give you the clothes that the Bichons stole for Julie! She's scared to wear them in front of her dads.

I can't believe you told her that the clothing was stolen!

Why not? It worked, didn't it? And now Jen has nice clothing, and it looks like she's doing you a favor by taking it.

Jen's Transformation

She wore the shirt as kind of a vest →

She cut the pants and made them into shorts

At least the belt looks kind of normal

I guess she liked the clothes.
Why can't we do anything right?
We have a new friend. That's good, right?
A new friend who looks like she was attacked by a weed whacker.

I just ran into Jen and she asked if we wanted to hang out this weekend at her house.

I have to ask my dads, but I'm sure it would be fine.

But GET THIS. Do you know where Jen lives?

No, but I'm sure Papa Dad wouldn't mind driving us there if your mom can't.

Jen lives right near Gretchen.

On the lake?

ON THE LAKE.

How is that possible?

Things We Learned From Hanging Out with Jen

① Jen doesn't dress bad because she's poor. *Because she's not.*

② Jen dresses bad because she likes to dress bad. *But why??*

③ Jen's parents have lots of money and her mom dresses really well.

④ Jen knows how to ride a horse.

I think we need to move to the next item on the Trunk List. *Agreed.*

We're going to skip Trunk List Item #3, Be Kind to People with No Friends, because we kind of sort of already did that with Jen.

Yay us!

Moving on now to Trunk List Item #4—

MAKE SURE ROLAND GETS CREDIT FOR HIS WORK

(IDEAS)

1. Tell Ms. Harrington.

Problem: that gets Jonathan in trouble, and then he'll hate us.

2. Make a brand-new Ash Lady comic and give Roland all the credit.

Problem: that's more lying. Also, I don't think my brain can handle another all-nighter.

3. Find a way to let the other kids at school know who really worked on the comic book.

goldstandard3000: I have a plan that is both totally brilliant and a little disgusting!

jladybugaboo: Okay, what?

goldstandard3000: When someone was mad with us, how did they let the rest of the school know?

jladybugaboo: They wrote bad things about us on the bathroom walls.

goldstandard3000: Exactly! Now what if we turned the tables and wrote good things about Roland on the bathroom walls?

jladybugaboo: But that's graffiti.

goldstandard3000: But would it really be so bad if it had a positive message?

jladybugaboo: I guess not. But this is stupid, because Roland would never see it.

goldstandard3000: He would if it was in the Boys' Bathroom.

jladybugaboo: But we'd have to go into the Boys' Bathroom to do it! That's totally disgusting!

goldstandard3000: And a little brilliant.

How to Get GRAFFITI in the Boys' Bathroom
(when you are not a boy)

OPTION 1: Get a boy to do it for us.
But which boy?

Jamie Burke?

Chuck Cavelleri?

Problem: You can't ever trust what Jamie is going to do.

Also, he has really terrible handwriting.

Problem: I'm not allowed to talk to Chuck anymore.

That is so irritating.

You're telling me.

I don't know anyone else that we trust.

Then we're going to have to do it ourselves.

PLAN A
FOR GETTING INTO THE BOYS' BATHROOM

STEP 1: Get convincing boy costumes.

Hallo. I am named Yevgeni. I am a boy.

STEP 2: Tell peopl that we are new foreign exchange students.

STEP 3: Go to the Boys' Bathroom without anyone ever knowing that we are actually girls!

I am Igor. I go to bathroom now.

This is a terrible plan. Agreed.

PLAN B FOR GETTING INTO THE BOYS' BATHROOM

We sneak in during class, when it's least likely for any boy to come into the bathroom.

But it has to be when we're in different classes because teachers never let two people go to the bathroom at the same time.

May we please be excused?

NO.

It's like they don't trust us.

We decided that the best time to sneak into the Boys' Bathroom was while I was in Spanish class and Lydia was in French.

I never thought that learning another language would come in so handy.
And then... there we were.

We had just taken out our markers
when the door began to open, so
we ran into the handicapped stall.

And then we saw this—
And then she'll say, "What does that mean, I look nice?"
Dude.
Yeah.
Dude.
Yeah.
Dooood. Break up with Jane already, this is getting old.

Perhaps we shouldn't have tried to graffiti the Boys' Bathroom during Chuck's lunch period.

You think?

After Chuck and Jim left, we quickly wrote on the wall.

WITHOUT ROLAND THERE WOULD BE NO HALVOR

But then we had to hide for another five minutes because someone else had to go to the bathroom

MINI-EXPERIMENT: Do All Boys Smell Bad?

What are you doing?

Nothing. Smelling your clothing. Nothing.

Honey, our child is being weird.

Again?

CONCLUSION: Boys who are related to me smell okay.

goldstandard3000: So what are we going to do about Chuck and Jane?

jladybugaboo: Excuse me? Are we supposed to do something about that?

goldstandard3000: Yes! Chuck is our friend. He's unhappy with Jane. We should help him.

jladybugaboo: You just want to help him to break up with Jane so that you can be friends with him again.

goldstandard3000: If being friends with Chuck again is a happy result of him breaking up with Jane, I'm okay with that.

jladybugaboo: Crazy lady. You have to stay out of his business. We have to stay out of his business. If he breaks up with Jane and then starts hanging out with you, do you know what that makes you?

goldstandard3000: What?

jladybugaboo: A BOYFRIEND THIEF.

LET'S PLAY THE **IF/THEN GAME**

IF Chuck breaks up with Jane...

THEN *Chuck will be happy!*

IF you talk Chuck into breaking up with Jane...

THEN *Chuck will be friends with me again.*

IF Jane thinks that you convinced Chuck to break up with her...

THEN *Jane will hate me even more.*

And say you're a Boyfriend Thief.

To anyone who will listen.

Guess who just talked to me!

Was it Roland?

It was! How did you know?

I saw him talking to you. What did he say?

He said, "Excuse me."

Do you think he saw the graffiti?

Maybe! Or maybe he just needed to get by me.

Whatever, it's a start!

Something weird is going on with the boys at our school.

Jamie, can you tell us the name of the first colonial settlement?

Without Roland there would be no Halvor!

It started with Jamie, so we didn't pay it much mind, but now all the boys are saying it.

You do the homework?

Without Roland there'd be no Halvor, man.

It's become like a weird code phrase or something.

But what is it code for?

Now everyone is saying it all the time. It's like this huge joke that everyone likes but no one really understands.

Are you thinking about running for student council again?

True.

You know, without Roland there'd be no Halvor.

Someone just wrote it on the wall in the Cafeteria!!!

I've been thinking, it's actually kind of cool that everyone likes what we wrote.

I guess it's good that Roland is getting the attention he deserves for working on the comic book, but vandalizing the cafeteria is too much.

I totally agree, but it's not like we did it. What we did do was come up with a cool catchphrase that everyone loves.

I don't think I like where you're going with this...

I'm just saying that we should get credit for it.

Oh no. No no no. We can't let anyone know that
a) We committed acts of Vandalization
b) We were in the Boys' Bathroom
We must NEVER EVER tell ANYONE.

I kind of already did.

My Portrait of Lydia Being A BUTT

goldstandard3000: Hi!

goldstandard3000: Hi!

goldstandard3000: Hi!

goldstandard3000: Are you online? It looks like you're online.

jladybugaboo: I'm online, I'm just not chatting with you.

goldstandard3000: How about now?

jladybugaboo: Nope, still not chatting with you.

goldstandard3000: But you just wrote back, so you are technically chatting with me.

jladybugaboo: I'm about to technically shout at you. WHY DID YOU TELL CHUCK THAT WE ARE WEIRD GIRLS WHO HANG OUT IN THE STINKY BOYS' BATHROOM?

goldstandard3000: I'm sorry, I should have talked to you about it before I said anything to Chuck. But don't worry, he won't tell anyone.

jladybugaboo: What if he tells Jane?

DISCOVERY!

If you want to keep a secret, don't tell anyone.

DISCOVERY #2

If you happen to tell someone don't tell someone who is in a romantic relationship, because peop in relationships hang out with eac other all the time and run out o things to say, so they have to te their partner EVERYTHING just keep from being bored.

So... I found out who started the whole "Without Roland there is no Halvor" thing...

WHY ARE YOU STILL TALKING TO HER? AND HOW DARE YOU MENTION THAT STUPID TROLL!!!

DISCOVERY #3

f you have to tell your secret to omeone who is in a relationship, ake sure they're not in a relationship ith THE SCHOOL'S BIGGEST LABBERMOUTH WHO HATES YOU.

You know who vandalized the Boys' Bathroom?

Candy Cane?

Lydia the Boyfriend Thief!

Okeedokey.

WHAT ARE WE GOING TO DO!???

It's only a matter of time before everyone in the school figures out some sort of horrible new nickname for us, and then we'll be branded with that nickname FOREVER!

EXAMPLES

BUGBOY

Brian Young: In 4th grade teacher found an ant colony in Brian's desk.

WIENER

Kelly Molloy: Ate nothing but hot dogs (without buns) for all of 3rd grade.

SWIRLY

Casey Parks: In 1st grade Casey stuck his own head down the toilet and flushed.

We began to work out some options
for how to handle our situation.

(1.) Move back to England.
What about me?

(2.) Move Julie and her dads
to England.

(3.) Get home-schooled.
Wouldn't one of our parents
have to quit their job to
stay home and teach us?
Do you have any better ideas?

(4.) Shave our heads, so that
we're known as "The Bald
Girls" instead of "The Boys'
Bathroom Girls."
HOW IS THAT A BETTER IDEA?

And while we were figuring out our options, Jen came over and asked what we were doing.

So you believe that if more people find out, you'll be shamed for life?

Yep.

Pretty much!

I like you guys. You're super silly.

Then Jen did the craziest thing.

We spent the day waiting for people to start picking on Jen for going into the Boys' Bathroom. At first no one seemed to care.

Blah blah blah

Talking about other stuff blah

But then people started talking.

Mad Dogs was in the Boys' Bathroom!

I thought she only went on fire hydrants.

And then, everyone seemed to know.

But Jen really didn't seem to care.
at all.

I hate that everyone is saying mean things about Jen.

But why would she go into the Boys' Bathroom? Is she crazy?

I think she went in there to take the attention off us going there.

But we never asked her to!

No, we didn't, but I think we should try to help her.

How? We tried to help her before and that just resulted in some ruined clothing.

I have a different idea. But we'll have to be brave.

How brave? Like skydiving brave?

A little.

Skydiving seems stupid because you're just hurling yourself out of a plane and you could easily fall and fall and fall until you die horribly.

At least when we committed social suicide we died horribly with friends. Strength in numbers!

goldstandard3000: Hi loser!

jladybugaboo: Hi outcast!

goldstandard3000: Hi bottom of the food chain!

jladybugaboo: Hi lowest totem on the pole!

goldstandard3000: Hi lame-y!

jladybugaboo: Hi lame-o!

goldstandard3000: Hi lame-est!!!

jladybugaboo: Okay, gotta go, Daddy's calling me to dinner.

goldstandard3000: I bet it's going to be lame!

Seeing how we're now thought of as complete weirdo-loser girls, there's a lot less to worry about. What have we got to lose?

STUFF WE NO LONGER HAVE TO WORRY ABOUT

1. Dressing nice!

② Being nice.

③ Smelling nice!

You know, after Sukie's mom died, we said we weren't going to care about what other people thought, but we actually kind of did.

Well, now we don't. Jen is nice and quiet and a good friend. She does her own weird thing and if people are going to be mean to her, then I don't care what they think about me. I really don't.

I don't, either.

We, the undersigned, really don't care what mean people think about us.

Lydia Goldblatt   Julie Graham-Chang

Remember how we vowed to not care what other people think about us?

That happened yesterday, so yes. I still totally don't care. Do you?

No! But I've been called into a meeting with Principal Rao during 8th period and I think I should probably care about that.

WHAT? WHY???

I have no idea!

Do you think it's for vandalism?

I HAVE NO IDEA!!!

I'm coming with you.

I don't think that's allowed.

← my completely terrified face

Julie has been in Principal Rao's office for half an hour. I'm supposed to be doing my math homework, but there's no way I can concentrate.

POSSIBLE REASONS FOR JULIE TO BE IN THE PRINCIPAL'S OFFICE

1. Vandalism. Through complex forensic investigation, the janitors have linked the ink in the Boys' Bathroom to Julie's pen.

2. Maybe Julie won an award! For something.

3. Something happened to Daddy and/or Papa Dad! I need to calm down.

WORST 8th PERIOD EVER

When I got to Principal Rao's office, Jonathan and Roland were already there.

Ms. Graham-Chang, perhaps you can shed some light on a certain situation.

It has come to Ms. Harrington's attention that Mr. Craven's contribution to his independent study project might not have been substantial enough to warrant his grade.

Now we know that you helped him with it, and he did credit you, but did anyone else help you two out?

I may have panicked a little.
So... what makes you think other people were involved?
I had my suspicions. Then all of my students kept talking about it. And not to be ignored is the obnoxiously large message painted on the cafeteria wall.
Oh. That.
Yes. That.

Both Jonathan and Roland were looking RIGHT AT ME.

If you tell them, it will be all your fault when I fail the class.

This is your chance to tell them about how we worked on the Ash Lady Adventures together.

What was I supposed to do?

THINGS I DIDN'T DO

LIE

I have no idea what you're talking about.

DIE

Julie? You don't look so good.

CRY

Although I really wanted to and almost burst into tears.

WHAT I DID DO

And then I had to sit and listen to Jonathan arguing his case.

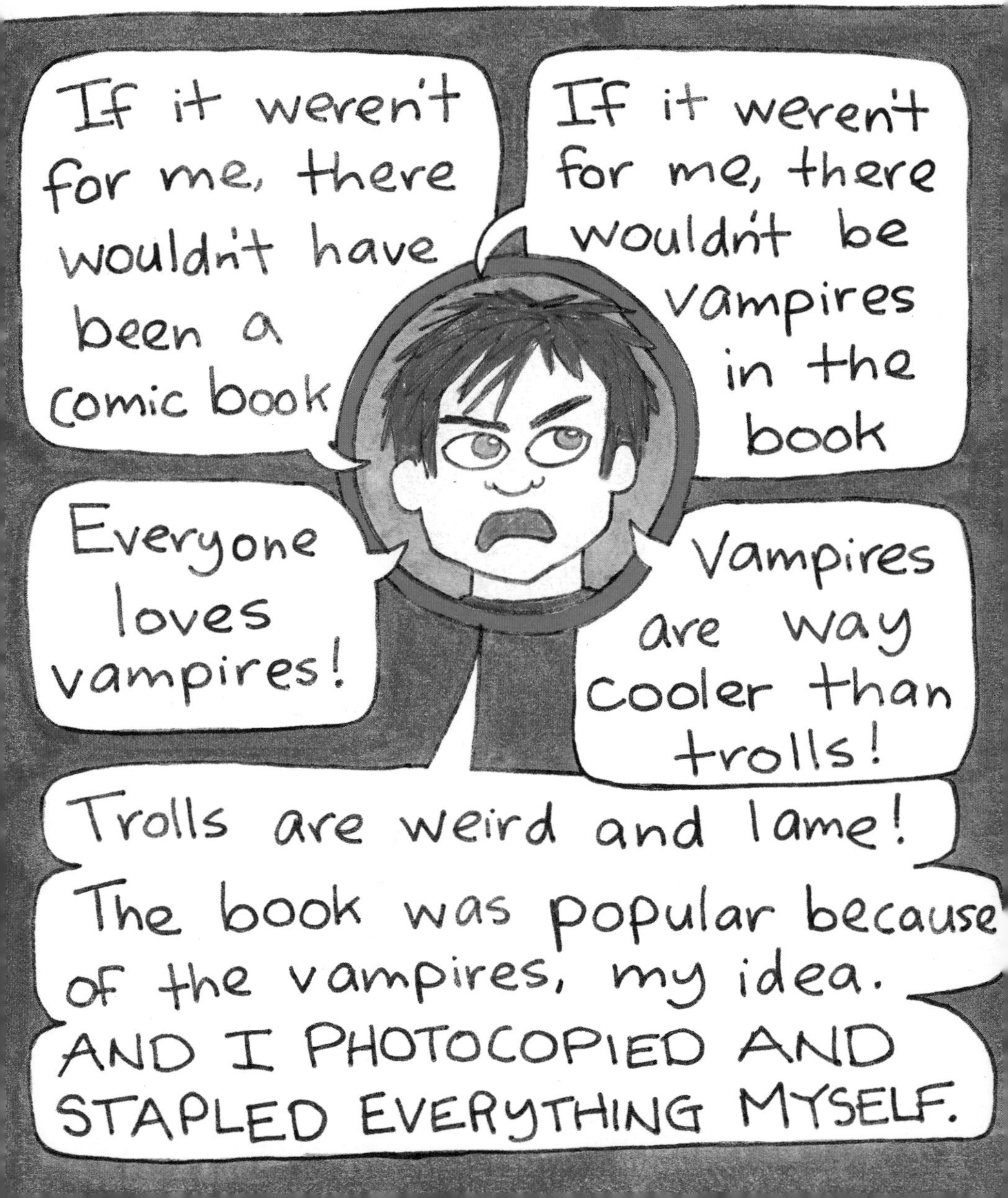

So now Jonathan's failed Art and is super mad at me, and Somehow Della Dawn found out.

Sorry things didn't work out with Jon. I guess he just figured out how lame you are. I could have told him that months ago.

But you know what? I feel better about telling the truth. Jonathan used me to get a good grade in Art, and that was really sort of a jerky thing to do.

Honesty is best.

Guess who I saw together?

Della Dawn and Jonathan? Roland already told me. Maybe they're perfect for each other after all.

From: jladybugaboo
To: sukiejaithoms100

So now Roland and I are friends again! He's helping me to carry my books to class, which is really great because Jonathan and Della Dawn are always cuddling RIGHT ON TOP OF MY LOCKER. It's pretty gross.

How are you doing? When are you coming to visit?

From: sukiejaithoms100
To: jladybugaboo

That's great that you and Roland are back together! I don't think I can visit anytime soon. After school is out my aunt is taking me to visit with relatives in San Francisco and I'll be there all summer. Want to come to San Francisco?

From: jladybugaboo
To: sukiejaithoms100

Just to clarify, Roland and I are back together as friends. Friendly friends who do friend things. Just friends.

I think I just did something maybe not so smart.

Maybe not so smart?

I just told Jane that Chuck wants to break up with her.

WHAT? WHY? HOW? Also, again, WHAT?

Look, I know we're not friends anymore, but I overheard something and I want to be honest with you because I always want people to be honest with me.

So then this happened

And then this happened

To: jladybugaboo
From: goldstandard3000

I really truly thought that honesty was the best policy! You were honest to Ms. Harrington and now you're friends with Roland again. I was just being honest with Jane.

To: goldstandard3000
From: jladybugaboo

I think that sometimes people don't want to hear the truth. Or maybe they're not ready to hear the truth, and they just have to find it out for themselves.

You know that things aren't going well when Melody thinks you look bad.

You look terrible.

Thanks.

What's wrong?

I told her everything that had happened with Chuck, and she was actually kind of nice to me and showed me how to knit a hat. I think I might be some sort of knitting genius, because it wasn't hard at all.

I'll draw, you stick to the fiber arts.

okay

I am _completely_ ~~sick~~
of Della Dawn!!!

What did she do now?

Just because she knows
something doesn't mean she
has to tell it to me. It's
none _of_ _her_ _business._

I think Della Dawn has a secret lair full of spy equipment that she uses to get dirt on everyone so that she can make them feel bad.

That seems unlikely, but she is really good at finding out what hurts you the most and then making sure that you hear it.

But why?

INFORMAL POLL

Why Would Someone Be Mean Just to Hurt Us?

Sometimes, when people hurt, they want to make other people feel just as bad.

I like to assume that mean people are just jealous of my beauty.

You may stop laughing now

Who is hurting you? Do I need to call Principal Rao?

Some people just suck. Avoid those people.

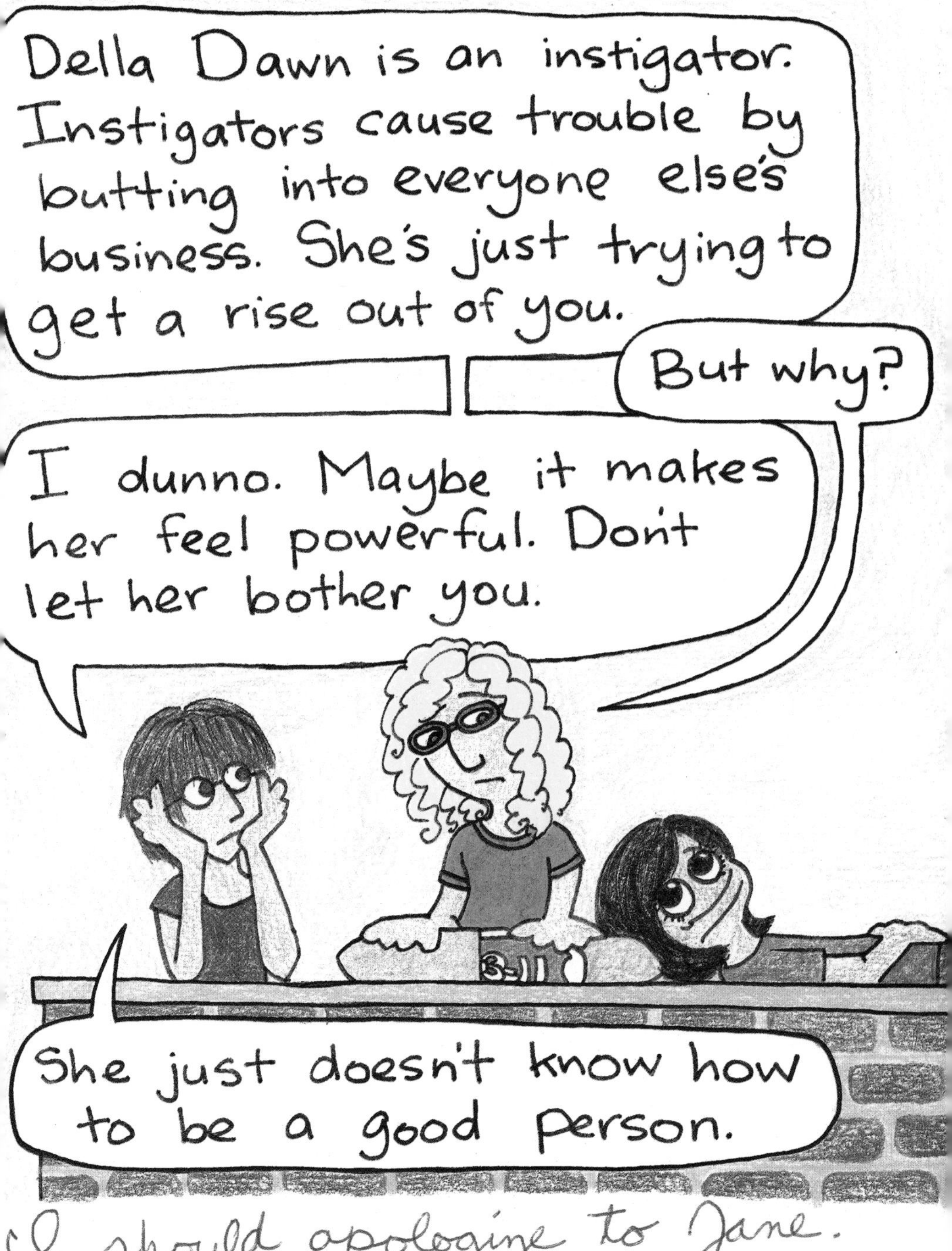

I should apologize to Jane.

REASONS for APOLOGIZING to JANE

1. I don't want to be the sort of person who makes other people unhappy on purpose.
     (like Della Dawn)

2. I don't want to be the sort of person who uses private information as a weapon.
     (like Della Dawn)

3. If I apologize, I'll prove that I'm <u>not</u> like Della Dawn.

4. I feel bad.

I'm sorry.

How did it go with Jane?

It may take her a while to accept my apology. But I'm glad I did it.

LAST WEEK OF SCHOOL!

All we have to do is survive the next five days and then we're done with 6th grade. FOREVER.

Nothing worked out like we thought it would. It never does, does it?

You will never believe what I just saw in the bathroom!

I DON'T WANT TO KNOW.

I DON'T WANT TO KNOW!!!

Nothing good ever comes from a story that starts: "You will never believe what I just saw in the bathroom."

You're really not going to believe it this time.

Lisa is the one who has been turning all the mean graffiti into flowers and designs and stuff.

We're totally grateful that you've been covering up the nasty things that people wrote about us, but why?
Sukie asked me to.
She never told me anything about it!
Maybe she thought you had enough on your mind already.

Lisa showed us an email that
Sukie sent her a while back.

From: sukiejaithoms100
To: princessmeowkins

Hi Lisa,

Could you do me a really huge favor? Julie's been telling me
about some of the stuff that people have been saying about
her and Goldy, and I thought you might be able to help.
They're having a really tough time.

Thanks! Say hi to everyone else! I miss you guys a lot.

Love,
Sukie

Princess Meowkins?
I can't believe that
Sukie is worried about
us having a really
tough time after
all she's been through.

Lisa didn't have to do anything for us. She could have just told Sukie that she was helping. Sukie would never have known if it wasn't tru

Lisa is a really good friend. And a good person, too.

Maybe being a good friend is how you become a good person. Like Jen

Hi.

Did you really tear up that shirt on purpose?

Yep. Want me to do any work on your clothes?

Dea god, n

Although maybe not everyone is mean to be friends with everyone else.

Do you think that Chuck and I will ever be friends again?

I don't know. Jane still hates us. And Jonathan is still mad at me. Maybe some friendships just aren't meant to be.

That sucks. I don't get it. We were honest, we tried to be good, and now no one likes us.

Except for Roland.

And Lisa, sort of. And Melody, sort of.

And Sukie.

And Jen, even though she's seriously weird.

So it could be worse.

And now we have the whole summer to figure out how to make it better...

Say what?

Acknowledgments

I am forever grateful to the wonderful staff at Amulet Books, who continue to astound me with their enthusiasm, support, understanding, and good humor. Thanks in particular are due to Susan Van Metre, Scott Auerbach, Melissa Arnst, Chad W. Beckerman, Chris Blank, Laura Mihalick, Mary Ann Zissimos, and the indomitable Jason Wells. Ever-lovin' thanks go to Maggie Lehrman, the best editor in the whole entire universe, who has always encouraged my love of hyperbole. Thanks to Stephen Barr and all the great people at Writers House, especially and always Dan Lazar, the greatest literary agent in the history of Ever. I have immense gratitude for all the friends and family members who have inspired me to write about friendship and family, for the fans who have given me wonderful feedback and encouragement, and for my dad, who reads my purple and pink books for kids. Last but not least, I give love and thanks to my best friend and favorite Phillies fan, my husband, Mark.

About the Author

Amy Ignatow is a cartoonist and the author of THE POPULARITY PAPERS series. She is a graduate of Moore College of Art and Design and also makes a decent tureen of chicken soup. Amy lives in Philadelphia with her husband, Mark, their daughter, Anya, and their cat, Mathilda, who just isn't very bright.

To my grandmother Gene Ignatow, who has made absolutely
certain that every bookseller and librarian in New Jersey
and southern Florida is well aware of my books and
the importance of keeping them in stock.
—Ig

Artist's Note: The materials used to create the book are ink,
colored pencil, colored marker, yarn, and digital.

PUBLISHER'S NOTE: This is a work of fiction. Names, characters, places, and incidents are either the product of
the author's imagination or are used fictitiously, and any resemblance to actual persons, living or dead,
business establishments, events, or locales is entirely coincidental.

Library of Congress Control Number: 2010930192

Paperback ISBN: 978-1-4197-0535-9

Text and illustrations copyright © 2011 Amy Ignatow
Book design by Amy Ignatow and Melissa Arnst

Printed and bound in China
12 11 10 9 8 7 6 5 4 3

Amulet Books are available at special discounts when purchased in quantity for premiums
and promotions as well as fundraising or educational use. Special editions can also be created
to specification. For details, contact specialsales@abramsbooks.com or the address below.

ABRAMS The Art of Books
195 Broadway, New York, NY 10007
abramsbooks.com